WHEN WE PRACTICE TO DECEIVE

A True-to-Life Novelette About Southern Life and Secrets

Written by L.L. Brown

ISBN: 978-1-7360697-3-8 (Paperback)
ISBN: 978-1-7360697-4-5 (eBook)

Cover Image by: Kinglion Online

Printed in the United States of America

Robinson Anderson Publishing
2150 S. Central Expressway, Suite 200
McKinney, TX. 75070

Table of Contents

"*When We Practice to Deceive*"

A Short Story by L.L. Brown

Everything was happening too fast. She stood in the mirror haunted by the memory of the old folks saying, "What's done in the dark *will* come to the light." Well, that light was getting closer and closer, and now it was coming too fast for her to stop it or outrun it. She could not believe it had been almost 35 years…

1.

In the Beginning

⟡

Back in the day, when we were "colored" and living in the "upper crust" world was the most coveted honor, reputation was everything. Whatever it took, we had to grow it, guard it, and protect it by any means necessary. Whether you were a teacher, postal worker, deacon, Mason, Eastern Star - whatever your status was in that bourgeoisie or, as it was more commonly known, "bou-gee" world - you did whatever it took to maintain it. Women held their heads high, children behaved, and men were gentlemen in suits and shiny cars, whenever they could afford them. Nothing was out of place for the "bou-gee" and nothing, but the best would do.

The Douglas' were a conservative Black family - "bougee" in every sense of the word. Carl Douglas had a prominent job working at City Hall as a building inspector and his wife Naomi was a woman of means and had her place as a member of the Order of Eastern Star, a secret society open only to the elect. She owned and operated the only Black grocery store in Ford and was so "bou-gee" that even the white folks in Ford called her "Miss Naomi."

Carletta Mari, her daughter, was a smart girl who respected her parents and was grateful for the luxuries their lifestyle afforded her. Her thick curly hair, perfect skin, and large hazel eyes made her stand out among all the young women in Ford County. She was the picture of what was considered beauty at that time when our attitudes about such things were still twisted by the painful legacy of slavery. She was absolutely stunning to all who beheld her and was the apple of her father's eye. But as every young girl does, she became distracted by a boy - a young man - whose every word she clung to.

Malcolm Thomas, the tall, handsome store clerk who worked for her mother was the finest man Carletta had ever seen! He was smart and kind and knew what he wanted. Even though he was from a much different place than Carletta, they had a lot in common. Malcolm's dream was to save enough money to help his mom move back to Philadelphia to be with her family, and to be able to attend Howard University. He was strong and determined and Letta was absolutely smitten with him. When he looked at her, her heart raced and when he said, "Hi, Miss 'Letta," in his thick southern drawl, she nearly swooned. Their exchanges were quick, stolen glances and greetings, until they weren't. From spring to summer, hellos turned into notes and then to secret meetings after dark. One thing led to another, and Carletta Mari "got in trouble." Well!

Carl and Naomi were "too through" with Carletta for getting into trouble, ruining their good name, and shaming Ms. Naomi. Why, she could never go back to her Eastern Star Sisterhood - the disgrace would be unbearable! And talking of love and marriage to the stock boy? This was foolishness of the highest degree. Love was a luxury. She would find love with the husband chosen for her and he would certainly have a pedigree that matched hers. Letta had lost her mind but this devilment would not stop Naomi.

2.

The Web is Woven

Being the kind of woman she was, Ms. Naomi did not hesitate for a minute. She had a plan and intended to carry it through. Bethel Mae, Naomi's oldest sister, lived in Cheneaux County some 500 miles away. BethMae, as she was called by her sisters, was a tall, strong woman with a stern hand and soft heart. Naomi knew she could count on her to help handle this "unfortunate" situation, so she called her big sister to come to the rescue. This was the only logical, safe choice in Naomi's mind, and one that so many women before her had chosen. She never thought she would be in this position, but suddenly she understood so well her classmates, relatives, and friends who took long visits to relations in far-flung towns and came back changed. She knew what she had to do. It was settled. She would take Carletta to Cheneaux County and BethMae would "handle" the trouble and everything would be alright.

Everything would be far, far away from Ford and from the world Ms. Naomi fought so hard to protect.

Carletta was heartbroken and ashamed. She loved Malcolm and wanted to marry him and have their baby but Ms. Naomi would rather have hosted a Klu Klux Klan lynching party than to have her world shattered by having a daughter "in trouble" (by a stock boy no less) and have her name shamed and disgraced. She would never stand for Carletta to marry a common laborer; not with her plans of Carletta attending Spelman, becoming a teacher, and marrying a man of means. After all, she was the only daughter of the Douglases of Ford County, and had a legacy to carry on, and it certainly DID NOT include the stock boy from the grocery store!

Letta's father, Carl, was a tall, handsome "paper-sack tan" man with hair that was "just good enough." He loved his "Letta" more than life itself, but more importantly, he was deathly afraid of Naomi or "Oni" as he called her. There was no discussion. The plan was set, and whether or not he agreed with "Oni's" decision, they had a job to do.

As he loaded the car with Carletta's things, Carl gave her a loving glance which said everything would be alright in his own way. He wanted his daughter to be happy, but he KNEW better than to cross Oni. As he was saying his good-byes to Letta, he slipped her a $10 bill and told her "not to worry." Carletta fought hard to hold back the tears and faked a soft smile to let her Dad know that she was sorry and that she did not blame him for what her mother was about to do.

And just like that, on Saturday morning before daybreak, Carletta and Oni slipped away on their long, silent trip to Cheneaux County. At first, Carletta tried to reason with her mother, but it was useless. She pleaded with her that she and Malcolm would get married *and* that she would not be disgraced, *and* that she wanted her baby, *and* that she and Malcolm were truly *in love*! A hard slap across her face which almost blinded her shushed this foolish talk, and she quickly saw Naomi's point of view - it WAS best for everyone.

The drive to Cheneaux took 10 hours. Carletta was thinking to herself - 10 hours - with her! Is this what HELL is like!!! She dreaded the long ride and the long, harsh talk that was to come. Carletta was silent after trying to plead her case; she did not dare to part her lips for fear of harsh retaliation for all of her transgressions since the beginning of her life! She stared hopelessly out of the window...praying, apologizing to God, and just hoping it would all go away.

After what seemed like hundreds of miles, Carletta thought, "This isn't so bad. Mother must be tired or just too mad to talk. Whatever the reason - thank you, Jesus!!! Driving down this long, desolate highway gave Carletta time to think. Was this legal - what her mother was doing? Girls were having babies every day! She still planned to go to school and fulfill Naomi's dream of her going to Spelman and becoming a teacher - all of that was still part of the plan. Why couldn't she have her baby, be with Malcolm, and fulfill her obligation to her mother? They could move far away from Ford County so they wouldn't disgrace the precious Douglas name. That seemed reasonable to her but she didn't dare speak it to Naomi. Instead, she just stared out the window and prayed that the trip would end soon.

As they crossed into Monroe County, Naomi looked over at Carletta, who was almost asleep and said in her meekest voice, "You wanna stop, Letta?"

Carletta was shocked that her mother even spoke to her and in a somewhat civil tone, no less.

"Sure. I could go for a drink and some chips." That was not the thing to say.

Naomi's voice became bold, harsh, loud and evil. "Chips and soda? You can forget that. You are pregnant now, and you will not be eating that shit, and Bethmae will see to that! You made the choice to get pregnant, so I will make the choice of how to handle it!"

By this time, Letta was so outdone with the outburst made by her mother she just sat in the car staring into space totally forgetting that she did have to use the restroom. The angry honk of her mother's car horn snapped her back to reality. She got out to go to the restroom and to get a drink. Naomi followed her inside to get fruit and juice and returned with some sort of hot sandwich, the smell of which made Carletta sick!

Naomi was getting tired. The drive was almost coming to an end, and she was restless. Bethmae was not the kind to "skate around" with. She would want to know the truth about the situation, and Naomi had to get her thoughts together before coming face to face with her sister. Carletta seemed relieved when she saw the Cheneaux County sign. They would be there shortly and the real drama would start.

Surprisingly, Bethmae was on the porch waiting for them to arrive. Jack, her husband, had gone into town to get a few groceries and a newspaper. Naomi pulled up nervously to the large porch that led clear round BethMae's house. It was a beautiful old house, and Carletta loved coming there in the summertime to get away from the "city." As they approached, Bethmae stood up in her usual stance - hands on hips and legs planted in a wide stance - but this time, she had the warmest smile on her face. Carletta actually felt welcomed. Bethmae hugged Carletta so tight she almost lost her breath. "It's gone' be alright, baby girl, don't worry." With that, an overwhelming peace came over Letta and she knew she was in the right place.

Almost six months passed with no word from Naomi. Bethmae and Carletta never spoke of Naomi and her "sadity" ways. Carletta felt safe and loved with BethMae, something she had not felt since being separated from Malcolm. Oh my God, did Malcolm even know? She had to reach him. But how?

Her time was nearing. BethMae said the animals knew when the time was nearing and that they would let Carletta know. To Carletta, Bethmae was a combination between a sweet old nanny and a voodoo queen witch doctor, and she was never wrong. The weather was changing, and there was a chill in the air. Carletta had a restless night dreaming of Malcolm and what he must be doing and thinking about this entire mess!

"You want breakfast, baby girl?" Bethmae sang out to Carletta as she was taking the homemade biscuits from the oven. "I got hot biscuits and fresh butter with my own honey - Jack got it from the hives yesterday."

That sounded very appetizing, and Carletta wanted hot biscuits, but she could not move! She felt like she weighed a ton. Her back was hurting and the pain was excruciating! "Aunt BethMae, something is wrong with me - come quick!" Carletta was screaming with pain.

Bethmae sat the orange juice out and took three glasses from the cabinet. She glanced out the window and dried her hands on her apron. She pushed back the curtains and saw the clouds moving fast. "It's time," she said to herself, "it's time."

"Jack! Get the comforters from the loft. Hurry up...and call Sister Portis...tell her to come quick! Letta is ready! Hurry, Jack!"

BethMae got the comforters ready and placed the towels at the foot of the bed. Carletta was crying and scared. BethMae assured her that it would be over soon and that "everything would be alright." She rubbed Carletta's huge stomach. "Won't be long now, baby girl...it's almost over."

Sister Portis was a quiet-natured lady with long white hair and a round stomach who looked almost comical. She prayed over Letta and prayed and prayed. She was so gentle; Letta was overtaken with her and followed her lead. She pushed and breathed and pushed and stopped and pushed and cried. "Don't worry, baby. This is your first. Sometimes it's hard and sometimes it's easy - only the Lord knows."

At that very minute, Carletta pushed and had an incredible feeling of euphoria. "We got it, we got it, Jack, get the towels!!! Here he comes!" Letta heard the sighs of relief and knew everything was going to be alright. "Well, Letta, you got yourself a handsome boy - he sho' got good color - thank God for that," Sister Portis said.

"Good color???" Letta thought, "God help me!"

After the excitement and Jack almost crying when the baby boy was delivered, Sister Portis told Carletta to stay in bed for a few days and don't - under any circumstances - leave the house for six weeks - till her time passes. Letta nodded her head and smiled, and thanked Sister Portis.

When Sister Portis and BethMae went in the kitchen alone she asked, "Sister, he sho' got good color and good hair. Daddy white? Is that why yo' sadity sister brought that chile way up here to have it?" BethMae was stunned that such a sweet and kind old Sister would say something so foul even if it was not too far from the truth. But that was beside the point!

"Naw, Sister, just a high yellow nigger who thought he could have his way with my niece. We did what we had to do, for Carletta's sake and yes, for Oni. She is my *sister*!" Sister Portis did not say another word. With a knowing look, she got her hat, her wrap, and purse and gave BethMae a strong hug. Without looking back, she left just as quickly as she had come.

Jack walked into the kitchen and said to BethMae, "Wonder how long it will take that to get all over Cheneaux County? You know how Sister Portis is, BethMae. How we 'pose to keep this up?" BethMae closed her eyes, and tears ran down her face.

"By the Grace of God, husband...by the Grace of God!"

———•◆•———

It had been just about six weeks. Carletta was enjoying her baby boy, which she called Thomas, Malcolm's last name. She held him all day long and brushed his hair. "You gone brush all that baby's hair out chile! Put that brush down," BethMae would tell Letta in a sweet, joyful voice. Carletta didn't suspect a thing. She knew that her aunt loved her and would not hurt her and would not let anyone hurt her...but Naomi, that was a totally different story! Naomi WAS BethMae's little sister, and BethMae had an unshakable loyalty to her.

On Friday night, BethMae told Carletta to get her things together and that it was time to go home. Naomi and Carl would pick her up on Sunday. Carletta was nervous. What would she say to her father? Never mind her mother - her conversation would be very limited with her for sure! She could do this - she just needed to get Thomi's things together first, and everything would be all right. She had her things packed in the suitcase she brought with her and Thomi's things were in a large pillowcase. She was ready to face the music!

Late Saturday evening, BethMae told Carletta to come with her to evening service; she wanted her to meet someone. Carletta went and Jack watched Thomi, or rather, Thomi watched his Uncle Jack! After service, BethMae introduced Carletta to Sister Barbara Thibodeaux. She was a beautiful woman, with "good hair and good color." She looked to be about 30 or so. BethMae made some sort of excuse and dismissed herself to go to speak with one of the Elders of the Church. Carletta thought something was bizarre. She and Barbara walked into the fellowship hall at the church, just to get a drink. Barbara began to speak about things that Carletta KNEW Aunt BethMae had told her. Carletta got very uncomfortable. She told Barbara that she knew she made a mistake but that she was ready to accept her responsibility and take care of her child. Barbara explained to her that she knew exactly what she was feeling because she herself had been in the exact position that Carletta was in now. She stated that children were all fine and good when the time was right, and she told Carletta the time was NOT right for her. Carletta became agitated and wanted to leave. Barbara caught her hand and told her to be strong. "Everything happens for a reason, and everything will be alright," she said with a pitying smile.

On the way back home, Carletta told BethMae what happened with Barbara. BethMae, not making eye contact with Carletta said, "Listen to what she is telling you, baby girl - she knows. Trust me, everything will be alright. You are a beautiful, smart young girl with a very promising future. You don't need a baby to tie you down, We are doing what is best for everyone. Trust me. Jack and I will keep Thomi. We will raise him and take good care of him. That is what Naomi wants, and it IS what's best for you." Carletta nearly fainted. How could her sweet Aunt fall to her mother! How could she betray her that way? Carletta cried all night and held Thomi next to her heart.

"I love you so much Thomas, and I know I MUST do what my mother wants. I know Aunt BethMae will take good care of you and let no harm come to you. I trust her, and I know she loves me." She kissed Thomi's eyes, his hands, and his little feet as she passed her son and her life on to someone else.

All the way home, Carletta was silent. During the entire 10 hour drive, she spoke one time. She was heartbroken. She had lost Malcolm and now Thomi - the only part of Malcolm that she had. She was depressed, just thinking about having to give her baby away. She prayed constantly for peace. When she returned to Ford County, no one questioned where she was and what had happened. Malcolm had gone off to Howard University to pursue his Law degree. That chapter of her life was closed. It was time to move on. She left the next year to attend Spelman.

3.

Life Goes On

Atlanta was a long way from Ford County, and so was all of the hurt from her past. Letta was loving Spelman, and life was actually good! Communication with her mother was limited, but Carletta talked to her dad, almost twice a week. He was a wonderful father to her, and she did not blame him for the actions of her mother. Her mother was her mother...no matter what. Time passed, and wounds healed. Aunt BethMae took ill and passed away when Thomi was 3 years old. Naomi and Carl took him in as their newly "adopted" son. No one in Ford County was the wiser. It was hard for Letta at times, but one thing that gave her peace was that her son was home, and she could see him whenever she wanted to! BUT, she could not let him know who she really was - that was the agreement, and Letta knew she had to stick to her side of the bargain if she was to have any sort of relationship with Thomi.

Letta was doing great at Spelman. Her grades were outstanding. She had joined a sorority, Delta Sigma Theta, and life was great! She met a guy, William Langston, thoughtful and tall, DARK and VERY handsome. He could NOT know her secret...not yet anyway. The relationship blossomed and got serious right away. Before she knew what hit her, Letta was planning her wedding, and her life in Ford County was a chapter that was forever closed.

But what about Thomi? Should she tell William about her life in Ford County, or should she leave well enough alone? Besides, Thomas was growing up. He knew Naomi and Carl as his parents and her as his big sister. Was it fair to disrupt his life? Was it fair to her?

William and Carletta were a handsome couple. He was tall and dark-skinned from a lovely, "well to do" Christian family that lived up North. Naomi would be pleased as punch! Well, with everything except the "dark-skinned" part. Naomi herself was "high yellow" and wanted to "preserve her good color." She always wore huge bonnets and hats during the hot months - so that the sun wouldn't darken her "good skin." It annoyed Carletta so much, but she knew her mother was her mother, and there was nothing she could do about that. What she could do was elope! If she didn't have a big wedding, with everyone from Ford county as her guests, she would save herself the embarrassment of her mother meeting William and his "dark skinned" family and listening to that mess about "good color and good hair."

She talked to William about it, saying that with everything going on in their lives right now, trying to plan a big family wedding in Ford County was just too stressful. He was disappointed because he wanted to bring the families together and have a huge wedding. He offered to pay. Carletta became angry - that wasn't the issue - but she couldn't tell him about the "color" issue, let alone about Thomi - especially not Thomi - she would when the time was right but not NOW. Carletta loved William, and she wanted to be with him. She had already lost Malcolm, but she was NOT going to lose William!

Saturday night was always Letta and William's special night. Something was going on with William, but Letta could not figure it out. He seemed very anxious. After dinner, William told Letta that he had to stop by the church. He had promised Father Robert that he would look at some financial papers that he needed to sign but wanted William to look them over and give his "expert" opinion. William was so smart! He was going to law school and would be joining his father's law practice when he graduated. Letta knew they would have a good life. She would never have to return to Ford again and never have to worry about losing William. Starting over up North was so exciting to Letta! She could finally be far away from the past that haunted her.

Letta told William that she would stay in the car because it was raining and she did not want to catch a cold. He pleaded with her to come inside - it would not take but a minute. Letta agreed. As they walked down the aisle toward the rectory, William pulled her into a pew and got on one knee.

"If you want to elope, we can. Point is, I love you, and I want us to get married right away. My father is getting old and is ready to retire. He wants me to transfer to finish my degree at home and immediately go to work at the firm. So whatever you wanna do - let's do it now." Letta was so happy she almost lost her breath! This was just what she had been praying for. A new life and a fresh start far away from Ford and Naomi.

The pressures of perfection had become a burden far too heavy to bare. She loved her parents, but Letta reeled at the idea of returning home and facing her mother. Traumatized by her disapproving gaze, and the weight of the secret they all bore, Letta simply could not risk the happiness she had fought so hard for. Walking on eggshells, hiding, and lying were not things she wanted intertwined with her new life with William. No. Thomi would be safe there and so would she. Like so many before her, she would run North towards freedom.

4.

The Web Continues

Naomi was nervous about flying. She pleaded with Carletta to come home to get married so the family could be there. When Letta sprang the news that they had to go ahead and get married because of William's dad being sick and needing to retire, Naomi was silent.

"Well, I guess I understand. Just when are we going to meet this handsome son-in-law of ours?"

"Soon, Mother, I promise. As soon as we get settled in our new home, we'll send for you and Daddy and Thomi. I promise."

Deep inside her heart, Naomi fumed. She wanted a big wedding for Letta where the whole town turned out with gifts. Was she pregnant again? Why did she elope? "I'll get to the bottom of this, if it's the last thing I do," she vowed.

Thomi was growing like a weed. He was eleven years old and as smart as a whip! He was beginning to show signs of "Letta" and people were beginning to "wonder and speculate." Naomi became withdrawn from her "bou-gee" society world and devoted her time totally to Carl and Thomas. Communication with Letta and William was infrequent. Naomi would always expect a phone call in October, Thomas's birthday, and in December, for Christmas. Thomi could always expect something wonderful from his "big sister" for both occasions and he often asked about her.

Almost three years passed and Ford was a closed chapter. Letta and William were happy. He was in school, finishing up his training and getting ready for the bar exam. He was already working part-time at his father's law firm. Letta was working part-time at Harrold's, the exclusive ladies clothing store where William's mother shopped. Everyone there loved Letta, and she loved her job! But, she had made a promise to William and herself that she was going back to school in the fall to pursue her degree in education because she still had dreams of teaching school.

The house was quaint and comfortable. Letta felt safe in her own world with William, but why was she always feeling ill? For the past three months, Letta had just about every bug you could imagine - cold, upset stomach, whatever. She had been as sick as a dog! Her friend from work, Sinclaire, told her to go to the doctor to make sure there was not something seriously wrong. Letta did.

That night, when William got home, he was surprised. The lights were low, the coffee table was set with candles, there was soft music playing, and the whole house smelled of his favorite food. He walked through the foyer, calling for Letta. She was in the sitting room on the sofa crying. "What's wrong, baby?" William asked.

Letta sobbed even harder.

"I wanted to make sure everything was perfect. I cleaned the house, I made your favorite food, I got our favorite wine, put out the candles, and everything! I wanted it to be perfect!" William was trying to make sure he said the right thing because he had no idea in hell what was wrong with Letta!

"Everything is perfect...you ARE perfect...what's wrong? Why are you so upset?" Letta took a deep breath.

"Because I took the casserole out of the oven, and when I saw it and smelled it, I threw it in the trash! It made me sick!!!"

William thought, "Okay, should I ask why it made her sick, or should I just acknowledge what she's saying?"

"Well, why did you get sick?"

"BECAUSE I'm PREGNANT and I was making a special dinner to celebrate!"

"Did you say pregnant...CARLETTA ...did you say PREGNANT?!" William screamed as he picked Letta up and swung her around, kissing her all over.

"Yeah, we're pregnant. Are you happy?" William, by this time, was crying and just overwhelmed with joy. He had been praying for a child, unbeknownst to Letta. "Baby, I am SO happy, I can't describe it. Just know that I love you, and I love our baby, and I just want to take care of you forever!"

5.

The Web Thickens

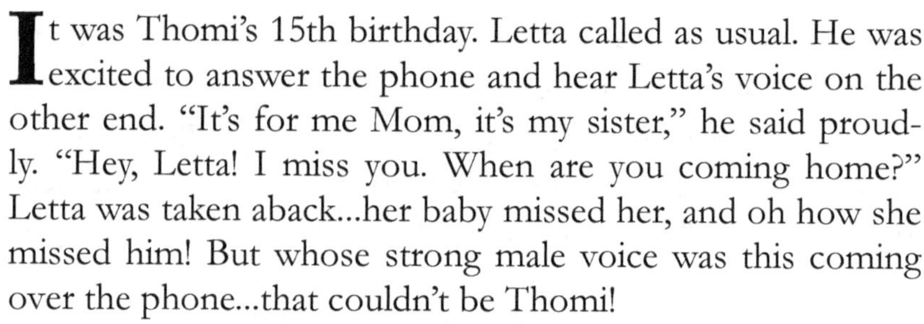

It was Thomi's 15th birthday. Letta called as usual. He was excited to answer the phone and hear Letta's voice on the other end. "It's for me Mom, it's my sister," he said proudly. "Hey, Letta! I miss you. When are you coming home?" Letta was taken aback...her baby missed her, and oh how she missed him! But whose strong male voice was this coming over the phone...that couldn't be Thomi!

She had to gather her thoughts. "Well, I am coming to see you soon. Happy birthday! I put something really special in the mail for you."

"Okay, thanks, Letta. I told my girlfriend we would go to the movies because my sister always sends me money for my birthday. I love you, Letta! Bye! Mom, Letta wants you!"

"Well, hello Mrs. Langston, how are you and William doing? I knew you'd call before it got too late. You know Thomas was waiting!"

"Ma, I need to tell you something."

"Oh Lord, are you okay? Carl come quick...something is wrong with Letta!"

"Mother, calm down, nothing is wrong. As a matter of fact, things couldn't be MORE right." Naomi was silent. She didn't know what to expect. "We're pregnant, Mother. William and I are expecting a baby." Dead silence.

Finally, Carl shouted into the phone, "Baby girl, that's wonderful! We are so happy for you and William. When are you coming home? We haven't even met him yet, and now we are having a grandbaby. When are y'all coming?" Letta felt their love and the weight of her absence and started crying all over again.

William took the phone. "Hey Carl, how's it going? We are doing good, just so excited about the baby. Tell Naomi she is going to be the youngest-looking grandma in Ford County!"

Naomi was speechless. She sat down on the chaise and stared out of her vast bay window into the night sky. "A grandbaby?" she thought, "Thomas will have a..."

Naomi entered into another "zone." It was like she had had a stroke and could not move or speak. Carl congratulated his baby girl, and said good night and that they were all excited and could not wait to see them soon!

"Now, Oni, why didn't you say something to Letta? She was so excited. You should have said SOMETHING!"

"A grandbaby," Oni whispered, "a grandbaby." Thoughts of the past entered into Naomi's mind and for a moment, she came to the reality of her own doing. She already had a grandbaby. The truth of the past had overshadowed her happiness. She reminded herself that she did what was best for her family at the time. She prayed and asked God to help her finally find peace with that decision. She looked at Carl and smiled. It was like he knew her inner thoughts and felt the same. "Well Carl, I know I'm not gonna be called granny. Mrs. Douglas will be just fine!" They both laughed out loud, a sound that they hadn't heard in some time.

Lord, What a Wicked Web We Weave

The nursery was so beautiful! Carletta prayed for a girl, and, of course, William wanted a son. Letta was progressing well with the pregnancy. They were both anxious with anticipation. Everything was ready and on time, and everyone was eagerly awaiting the blessed arrival. Letta would often stand in the mirror naked, rubbing her stomach and talking to her precious, unborn child. "You are so special and so very, very loved. Nothing and no one will ever take you away from me."

On one such occasion, William had come home early to take Letta shopping for baby clothes. As he entered the bedroom he overheard Letta saying, "Nothing and no one will ever take you away from me."

"Hey Babe, how y'all doing?" William's sexy voice startled Letta.

"What had he heard?" she thought. "Oh My God...What did he hear?"

"Are you ready to go?" His face was puzzled, but he didn't say a word. He wondered what her words meant but also was accustomed to Letta's far off and dreamy thoughts. Sometimes she seemed a world away from him and it was often difficult to tell what she was thinking.

"You startled me, William! Yes, let's go. I've been waiting for you all day!" Letta said breathlessly.

When they arrived at the mall, it was crowded, and the mix of emotions Letta had just torn through had wiped her out. Still, she had to prepare. Everything had to be perfect.

Within a few hours, William had a gazillion bags in his hands, and they were both worn out. "Can we eat now, Honey? I'm exhausted, and my feet are killing me."

William was deep in thought and didn't hear her at first. "William Langston! Do you hear me, boy?! I'm about to faint from hunger."

"Oh, sorry, Letta. I just...Letta, why did you say what you said...earlier, at the house?"

"What are you talking about?" she asked, suddenly feeling nauseous and light-headed.

"Letta, when I came into the bedroom this afternoon, you were in the bathroom, talking to the baby and I heard you say, 'Nothing and no one will ever take you away from me.' What did you mean, Letta? Why did you say that? Are you scared about something? Trust me, nothing is going to happen to our child, and no one will ever harm our child. I pledge my life on that."

He hugged Letta, and she closed her eyes. How could she have found someone so sensitive and wonderful? Should she tell him the truth? He didn't deserve to live with a lie, but she couldn't bear the thought of losing him and her perfect little family right when she was about to give birth. No, William would never need to know, and she would have to take her secret to her grave. Everything would be alright.

6.

A Blessing and a New Beginning

"**P**ush, Letta! Push, baby! We're almost there!" Letta was having a hard time. She thought to herself, "I knew I gained way too much weight. God, help me!" The birthing nurse was trying to get Letta to relax, but she couldn't. She was scared, anxious, happy, and just a basket of nerves!

"Relax, Mrs. Langston! Please! It will make everything so much easier. Oh! I see the crown! Just relax and when I say push, push with all your might, okay?" Letta was ready. She wanted to see her baby and give it all the love it could. "PUSH...here it comes...here it comes...look at that beautiful baby BOY! He's a big one, Mrs. Langston! Congratulations!" William was beside himself. A boy! YES!!! William Thurgood Langston III had arrived!

"Letta, he looks like you, but he's got his Daddy's beautiful dark skin," the nurse said. Whatever would her mother think? Letta fainted!

When they arrived at home, Sister Carver was already at the house waiting to greet them. "Lord, Lord, give me that baby! Mr. Langston, he is a big strong boy, just like his daddy was." Sister Carver was from the church and had practically raised William and his sister, Olivia. She was a highly educated woman who had taught at the Catholic school in town for many years. She was a fixture at every church gathering, and was William's mother's best friend and long-time confidante. "You get settled," Sister Carver said. "I'll take care of "Trey. William, you know your daddy has already given this child a nickname."

William laughed, "Yes, ma'am, I know. So I guess he is "TREY."

William and Letta had never discussed what happened at the hospital when Letta fainted, but William had to know. He knew Oni was color-struck, but could Letta be too? Blacks in the South were obsessed with color, and some in the North, too. It was like the caste system in India, where color could keep you in a "place" in life like a ball and chain. His father encountered it, and so had he. Even as an accomplished lawyer, he got odd looks in the courtroom and from people he passed on the street - Black and white. There were even Black social clubs, fraternities, and sororities where if you couldn't pass the "paper bag test" you couldn't gain entry. When would Black people be free of the vestiges of slavery? How could he make his son understand that he was beautiful just the way God made him, especially if his own mother didn't think so? William was a patient and understanding man, but he had to know. Was Letta disappointed? Old habits die hard, and he was far too accustomed to comments about his "dark skin" not to notice the precise moment when she fainted. "Letta-girl, you gave everyone a scare at the hospital! Did you get light-headed and pass out. What happened?"

Letta studied his face. She had to get her thoughts together. She was only worried about what Oni would think but she did not want to push her husband away during the most important time of their lives. She loved William and loved his gorgeous dark skin. But Oni…she just wanted to protect her baby from his grandmother's inevitable critique. Letta could hear her now, "Look at his ears, do you think he'll lighten up?" She couldn't imagine the horror of having Oni embarrass her in front of her husband and her in-laws who had been so kind to her. The world is so cruel. Her baby was only 3 days old and her heart was already bursting with fears, anxiety, and love for him. She vowed to protect him - to protect them all - even from Oni.

"I was just so overwhelmed, honey! Having such a beautiful baby, I was just overjoyed. That's all, honey. I'm fine - don't worry, everything will be alright."

7.

Home

Trey was growing like a weed! He loved to eat, and at just six months old he was huge! Anyone could see that he would be tall like his father, and definitely had his daddy's "color." On his 6 month birthday, the day had come for Trey to get out into the world so Letta and Willam had planned a trip to the movies. Letta's hands were full, changing Trey's clothes so that they could get there on time when the phone rang. "Get the phone, William!"

Within moments, Letta's heart stopped. She knew it was Naomi. Whenever William said, "Hello, gorgeous!" she knew it was her. "Oh Lord," Letta thought, she'll ask again, "When are you coming home?"

Letta had been dodging this trip and avoiding a visit with her parents with every excuse under the sun. When her in-laws asked when her parents were coming to see the baby, she told them they were busy with Thomi, and the store, and their social circles. She always had a ready excuse. Secretly, they wondered about this strange family who hadn't even bothered to meet them. Letta was a lovely daughter-in-law, but her parents sure seemed distant. William had told them they were "society" down south, so they assumed that Letta's parents thought their daughter was too good for William. Southern Blacks could be so uppity. Letta didn't realize that she had bred this contempt between their families, but then again, she didn't care. She had to protect her family - William and Trey.

"Mother, hi! How are you and Daddy and Thomi? What's going on?" Letta was almost afraid to hear the response.

"Oh, we are all doing fine. Thomi is playing basketball and working at Mr. Bolger's store. That's keeping Carl and I busy. I must admit - he is good at ball - he's fast! How y'all doing, and how's that beautiful grandson of mine? I thought you were sending pictures. You know, Carletta, (okay, here it comes, Letta thought) it's a shame and disgrace before God that we have not seen you in God knows how long, and now our grandbaby is probably walking and we haven't seen him yet! Girl, I should..."

"Mama, we are coming for Christmas! William has been so busy at the firm, but in December, he has three weeks off, so we will be there for Christmas - promise! You will be surprised when you see Trey. He looks like me, but he IS his daddy's son! It will be good to come home. We should be there the Tuesday before Christmas. I don't know how long we'll stay- maybe a week or more...so make sure you have some greens and dressing; that's what I want."

———— •◆• ————

Ford county was all dressed up for Christmas! Some things never change, Letta thought, as they took the fork in the road to get to Douglas House - what the folks in Ford called Carl & Naomi Douglas' home. Douglas House was an old plantation left to Carl's grandfather by his white father who was also his master. Removed by time from the horrors of slavery, it was now a historic home with beautiful grounds, a lovely walk-around porch, and immaculate interior. It reeked of Naomi! The South was such a twisted mess of beauty and trauma.

As they drove up, Trey was just waking up. "We're here, baby-boy! We are in Ford County!" Letta was suddenly hit with a flood of emotions. Could she handle this? Could she handle Naomi's judgmental comments?

"Carl, come quick! Letta 'em are here! Lord, Lord, my baby is home!!!" She could hear her all the way from the driveway. Sweat formed on her brow.

Letta felt 16 years old again. Her stomach tossed and turned. She had to get a grip...quick! She was an adult, and she would not let Naomi control her or make her feel like she was a failure. She was proud of her husband and her son and the choices she had made in life, and she would NOT let Naomi take that away. With a deep breath, she straightened her back and readied herself to meet whatever her mother might say with a smile.

"Welcome home, Baby... and well, well, well, Mr. Langston, finally we meet! You are as handsome as my daughter said. No wonder you stole her heart!" Naomi gushed.

"I'm in the Twilight Zone," Letta thought. "No joke about color? Is this for real?"

"Mother, you look beautiful! You've cut your hair. In the last pictures you sent your hair was so long!"

"...and GRAY! Naugh, chile, I thought I'd get it cut. They say it makes me look younger. Y'all come on in! Thomas had to take his girlfriend, Frei, to work. Chile, yes, that is her real name. Her parents are a bunch of Northerners. Smh!"

Letta thought, "Okay, here it comes! I knew she wouldn't let me down."

"Now, Mom, William is a Northerner. Don't say stuff like that."

"Yeah, but he's the father of my beautiful, beautiful grandson! Letta, he is a doll!"

"Okay, where is my mother? The REAL Naomi Boudreaux Douglas? This is definitely not her, Letta thought. Lord, what is going on in this house!"

"Listen to that boy - driving up to this house with that music blasting! Oni, I told you we shouldn't have gotten him that fancy car," Carl muttered as he peered out the window.

Letta couldn't believe her eyes! Thomi was at least 6'6! He jumped the porch and ran into the kitchen. "Where is she? Where's my big sister?"

"Thomas Carlton Douglas, you better come here and give me a hug!?" Letta had to fight back the tears. "Boy, you are grown! Look at you...taller than me!"

"Uh, excuse me, big Sis, but that wouldn't have to be too tall!" Thomi laughed as he grabbed Carletta and swung her around. "Letta, I missed you! I missed seeing your face. The phone calls and letters and the money were all good...but damn, it's good to see you!"

At the moment, Letta realized how many years she had missed with her son. He was a man now and his childhood had just slipped away while she was hiding from her mother. But Thomi was happy, healthy, and strong! She thanked God that Naomi and Carl had taken care of him and that he was doing well and that they had done well in raising him. She thanked God that everything was okay. This may not be the path she would have chosen, but, praise God, everything was okay.

"See what I mean," said Naomi. "You know better than to curse, boy, just too grown. Smh! Thomas has been a wonderful son - despite his mouth sometimes - and we are proud of him. We are very proud of both of our kids, huh, Carl?"

"You got that right, Oni!"

Christmas dinner was heavenly. Letta had missed her mom's cooking - and Oni could burn! Sweet potato pie, fruit ambrosia, greens, dressing, all of Letta's favorite things. "Mom, I'll help you with the dishes. Let's get the table cleared."

"Oh, baby, thank you, I appreciate that. We can have a little girl talk' in the kitchen."

"Was it coming now?" Letta thought, "Here we go."

"Boy, this water is hot! Girl, why did you use such hot water?"

"Good to cleanse your soul, Mother," Letta said without thinking first, as she had often done when she was at home. She had forgotten what it was like living in a house where you always had to think before speaking and were always afraid of what Oni would say and how she would react. Her mother was HER mother, and there was nothing she could do about that. But hey, she was a grown woman now with a loving husband, a beautiful home, and a precious baby. She didn't have to bow down to anyone anymore.

"Cleanse your soul indeed, chile, indeed," Naomi said as she dried the huge pot. "Yes, the soul does need to be cleansed from time to time, yes indeed."

Letta was through with the chit-chat. Emboldened by her own words, she said, "I was surprised you didn't pass out when you saw William and Trey, them being "dark-skinned" and all. I just knew you would faint!"

Naomi was silent. Letta could tell by the look on her face that she was shocked by what she had said. Letta prayed silently for God to guide her words. "I just meant, you used to always tell me to protect my "good color" and how the world was so unkind to our people who were "dark-skinned" and how Daddy's grandfather was a white man and how down through the generations, that "good color" had been tarnished and it was up to us to make sure we protected our "good color."

"Lord, chile, what are you talking about? Why are you talking about that? You think I don't like William or Trey because of the color of their skin? Lord, what kind of person would think a thing like that? What has the North done to you, Letta?"

Letta thought, "Did I totally misunderstand my mother all those years? Was it me who thought "good color" was important? What has happened?" Letta knew she had to get her father alone and find out what had "happened" to her mother because this lady was not Naomi Boudreaux Douglas!

Time and space changes people and situations. Oni missed Carletta and the times they shared. Naomi reflected on the choices she had made in her own life and how every decision she made was what she thought was the right and proper thing to do at the time. Her daughter was the most important thing in her life. Every decision made concerning Letta was what Oni thought was best for Letta. Oni's epiphany was that the decisions were made to protect and preserve the Douglas' reputation above ALL. Over time, acceptance of this brought a new awareness to Oni. She vowed to not make the same mistake with Thomi. Oni had changed. She had softened. Life had revealed to her what was important in her life and she lived her life to reflect that change.

Two weeks came and went, and soon it was time to go. Letta had enjoyed her stay, and William had finally met his other family. Thomi was leaving for work as Letta and William were preparing to leave to return home. "Well, Sis, I guess I'll check y'all later! Make sure you take care of my handsome nephew. Frei says he looks like me. You know I'm gonna have to teach him some "game!" Since y'all leaving so early, I probably won't see y'all, so Y'all be careful going back. Peace!"

Letta hadn't gotten past the fact that Frei said Trey looked like Thomi. To make matters worse, she had overheard her mom and dad talking that night when she got up to get a drink of water. "Carlton, that baby and Thomi could pass for twins. Can't you see it?"

"Of course I can see it, Oni! I'm worried now. Thomi is a smart boy. He will start piecing things together and asking questions. You know how he can ask questions. I believe it's time. But we have to talk to Letta and William cause it's obvious William does not know."

Letta thought, "Oh my God! I gotta' get back home to where I am safe."

Carletta was up early at the crack of dawn. The car was packed, and they were ready to get back to Chesterfield. "William, is everything in the car? It's time for us to get on the road."

"And back to my SAFE haven," Letta thought. "Away from the past and away from the deceit. Oh, what a wicked web we have woven!"

"I wish y'all could stay," Naomi said.

"Me too, Mother! We will see you again, soon! I promise."
They said their goodbyes and Letta, William, and Trey disappeared down the road.

8.

The Web Closes in

It was Valentine's Day, and Letta had to close the store. She had been busy all day helping husbands and boyfriends with gifts for their special ladies. She was thinking, "I wanna go out tonight! I think I'll call Olivia and see if she's free to keep Trey. She loves her nephew."

Fortunately, Olivia was free and agreed to come and get Trey and take him to the movies. Letta and William could have a lovely evening alone for a while. Everything was great! Letta had food delivered, so they didn't have to go out. She would plan a romantic evening at home - just her and her man!

The food arrived so quickly Letta didn't have time to finish getting ready. She put everything in the oven to stay warm while she ran upstairs to shower. William would be home shortly, and she wanted to be ready and waiting. When she heard the garage, she knew her man was home! "Hey, honey, how was your day? Happy Valentine's Day! Hope you're hungry."

William was excited as well. He had closed a big deal at the firm, and they had celebrated all day. He asked Letta if she had gotten his message. "No, I didn't check the machine," Letta said, "What's up?"

"Well, I had left you a message to ask if Olivia could babysit. I wanted to take you out and celebrate."

"Oh no, honey, I didn't get the message, and I already got takeout. I was kinda' thinking the same thing, so I already asked 'Liv to take Trey to the movies. BUT, we can always eat the take-out later. I'll get dressed!"

The evening was so nice! Kirby's was Letta's favorite place - it was filled with ambiance and class. Letta thought to herself, "The older I get the more I AM like my mother," she snickered to herself but her smile spilled over.

"What's funny? Share that thought with me." William said.

"Nothing," Letta said, "I was just thinking about something I saw on TV. More importantly, congratulations, baby! I'm so proud of you!"

After a beautiful dinner and two bottles of Merlot, Letta was very "happy." She talked about growing up in "Douglas House," and how at her debutante ball Johnny Mathis sang to her, and how she lived the "Douglas Life" for so many years but that being with William was the only thing that had brought her true happiness and love. "Nothing matters but you, Trey, and our life in Chesterfield," she said lovingly.

William beckoned for the check. He knew Letta was "tipsy," and they needed to get home so Olivia could get back to her own house before it got too late. On the way home, while

William was singing along with one of his favorite songs on the radio, "Just My Imagination," he suddenly startled Carletta.

"Letta, didn't you tell me that Thomi was adopted?"

"Yeah," Letta said, suddenly feeling sober. "Where is he going with this?" she thought.

"My mother adopted him from a teen mother," she said matter-of-factly. "Why?"

William said, "Oh nothing - it's just that every time I look at Trey, especially when he's really laughing, he looks so much like Thomi. Remember, I used to say Trey looked so much like you. I don't know...I just thought about it...I said the next time I thought about it, I was going to tell you...that's all."

Letta became so silent she could almost hear her eyelashes bat. She thought, "He knows...who wouldn't?!? Trey and Thomi DO look alike - almost like twins! Hell, they should... they ARE brothers!"

Letta was nervous and quiet the rest of the night and her mind raced - what should she do? How would William react? Would he understand? Maybe she just needed to start at the beginning and tell him the whole long story - everything. My, my, my, what a wicked…

—— • ● • ——

"Honey, get the phone! I'm getting out of the shower!"

Carletta could hear William from the bathroom. "Hey, little brother! What's going on? When? Sure, that would be great! You've never been up here, and I know your sister will be elated. Let me know your flight arrangements. We'll have to drive to Boston to pick you up - we're about 1 ½ hours away. I'm not going to tell Trey - he'll be so surprised - he brags to his friends all the time about his Uncle Thomi...Letta!

Come to the phone! It's Thomi. He's flying up here in a couple of weeks."

"Hey, big head - what are you coming up here for? Oh, so you're headhunting? Oh, okay. How long? Oh, that will be good. We can do some things while you are here...Have I talked to Mom? Yeah, I know. I sent her and Dad pictures of Trey. Yes, I have one for you! You are the man on the move. I never know where to send your mail, chile! Yeah, me too, okay. Tell Frei hello...take care...much love...bye!"

Carletta looked as pale as a sheet! "Lord, give me strength," she thought, "I have to tell William!"

9.

The Web Continues to Thicken

"Thomi is so handsome," Letta thought to herself, "I can see Malcolm in his eyes."

"Thomas Carlton Douglas! What in the world have you done to your head? What happened to all of that beautiful curly hair?"

"Letta, where have you been? Braids, my sista! Braids! Everyone in Atlanta has them. You need to ditch that perm and let your nature locs flow."

"William, she has beautiful hair!" Letta was startled when Frei walked in, and she immediately knew why her mother was so hard on Frei. She was a natural girl with lovely red locs! "You know what? I just might do that. Daddy used to love my hair before the PERM!"

Letta could not believe Thomi was almost 26 years old. He was grown and even thinking about getting married! Lord, what a wicked web we weave when…Letta's thought was interrupted by Thomi and Trey and their loud laughter. It was eerie. They sounded JUST alike! As they laughed, William smiled but stared at them quizzically. Letta's heart raced. Does he know? He's a smart man - surely he can't be fooled.

"Who's ready for a game of Monopoly?" Letta interjected to distract him from whatever he might be thinking. If he knew, she would wait for him to tell her. Letta thought to herself, is this the right time? How could she let this linger on? Should she tell William when Thomi leaves. Should she just lay IT all out and let whatever happens, happen? How long would this web of deceit continue. It was becoming apparent that Thomi and Trey were related somehow and William sensed something. "I want the car if we're playing Monopoly" William laughed out, bringing Letta back to reality…. Maybe now is not the right time.

Thomi's visit was over so quickly! Trey hated to see his Uncle Thomi go! These past four days had been great, and he couldn't wait for school to be out so he could go to Atlanta to see his uncle. He was really looking forward to that!

"Okay, baby, call me when you get home and tell Frei we said hi and let me know how she's coming on her dissertation. Tell her we are very proud of her. Be safe! Don't forget your book!" Thomi waved as he entered the tunnel to the airplane. He had enjoyed his trip and the training was good. It was great to see Trey and Letta, but he was ready to see Frei. They had not been apart for four whole days since they first started dating back in high school! He missed her smile and her beautiful red locks…she was his soulmate and he couldn't wait for her to be his wife!

Frei was making out her guest list. "Thom, call your sister! I need some addresses."

"Just call Mom - she has everyone's address."

"I know that, Thomas, but I DO NOT want to call Oni - excuse me, Ms. Naomi - she constantly gives me the blues. She hates me!"

Thomi fell on the bed laughing. "She does NOT hate you. She just wants you to straighten your hair. She's weird like that. When I was little, she always told my sister, 'Go get your hair fixed. I hate those nappy curls!' I guess it reminds her of a time she wants to forget and never ever remember. She's from that time."

"Thom, don't try to make me feel sorry for her. She's just like my Aunt Chez, just bou-gee, bou-gee, bou-gee! Besides, you love my hair, don't you, Thomi?"

Not only did he love her hair, but he also loved her eyes, her dimpled left cheek, and her crooked third toe. He loved all of her!

"Hi, William! Can I speak with Letta?"

"Hey, Letta! We're finally making the guest list, and I need some addresses...Yeah, I know, but I just wanted to hear your voice."

"Frei, you are just too sweet! I am looking forward to us being sisters," Letta said, the guilt seeping in as soon as the words left her mouth. Frei had also noticed and commented on how much Thomi and Trey resembled each other. "That girl is too smart for her own good," Letta thought, "I hope she doesn't start asking questions."

The web was thickening...this had to end. Letta had to face the music AND William.

10.

And in the End

It had been almost five years since Letta had seen Thomi and Frei after their wedding. She had sent them photos of Trey, and they had, in turn, sent her "pregnant photos." Frei was due in the fall, and Thomi was just beside himself. Letta had gotten so used to keeping her family at arm's length for fear they would undo her perfect world with William and Trey, that Thomi had grown accustomed to standing on his own. She missed him and wanted to get to know Frei - and her soon-to-arrive grandchild - but couldn't bear the questions, the gazes, and the moments when she was sure that some knew.

Besides, Letta had her hands full with Trey. He was dreading summer school, and his senior year in high school was much more challenging than he had anticipated. He needed to tighten up his "game." He did not want to explain to his

Uncle Thomi the C he got in calculus. Just as Letta was taking the clothes from the dryer, the phone rang. It was Naomi.

"Hey Mom, how are you guys doing? I was just thinking about Daddy. I saw that golf club he was talking about, and William and I were thinking about getting it for…"

Naomi interrupted, "Letta, Daddy had a heart attack. We're at the hospital. Aunt Carrie Jean and Uncle Benson are here with me. Your Daddy is really sick, and he is asking for his baby girl. I need you here, Carletta."

The blood rushed from her arm and Letta dropped the phone. She was dizzy and in disbelief. The silence was deep and dark.

William came into the laundry room when he heard the noise. "Babe, what is it? Who's on the phone?" He picked up the receiver as Letta dropped down at the kitchen table.

"Hello? Hey, Naomi. What? When? Okay, okay. I'll drive her to Boston, and she can get the next flight out. No, Trey will stay with me - he's never here anyway. You know how it is. Don't worry Naomi. Letta is on her way."

Letta thought to herself as the plane was landing, "I need my Daddy, I need my Daddy. Lord, please take care of my Daddy." Benson met Carletta at the airport. He looked much older than Letta remembered and she saw her Daddy in him - just a younger version. "Uncle B, how's my Daddy? He's gonna' be fine, right? He just needs to stop eating those pig feet, right, Uncle B?"

Benson Douglas was Carl's baby brother - well, almost. He was the "mixed" child of an illicit affair between Carl's dad and another woman in town, but Carl's mom accepted him and raised him as her own child - and he loved her for that. It was not Benson's fault that their "papa was a rolling stone." Benson loved Charlotte Douglas, and as far as he was concerned she was his mother. It takes a mighty large heart to ignore the talk in a town like that and raise the son of your husband's mistress.

"Baby girl, Uncle B has never lied to you. I'm scared this time. Smoky looked fragile and tired. I don't know. I'm scared."

Yeah, "Smokey!" She had forgotten that people in Douglas sometimes called her Daddy Smokey because he could sing like Smokey Robinson. He didn't look like him in the least bit - but he sounded JUST like him and could make the entire church shout on Sundays. Letta smiled to herself as she reminisced.

By the time they got to the hospital, the whole town was there. Carl and Oni knew a lot of people - almost everyone in Ford County - and they had all showed up! Oni hugged Letta and said, "Your Daddy's waiting. He needs to see you...now Letta...now."

Carl looked like a small old man shrinking right before Letta's eyes. What had happened to her father? Where was the tall, handsome man with the beautiful "salt and pepper" hair? What happened to his dimples? His eyes were light brown - not yellow. What was happening? It was then that Letta realized that her Daddy was SICK, and she knew it was not good. "Hey, Daddy! I'm here, I'm here, Daddy! I love you!" she cried.

Carl was weak. His eyes were sad and unfocused. He whispered as he spoke, "Letta, you still look like my mother... everyone used to say, 'that baby looks like Ms. Charlotte,'... you look like Mama..." Letta knew her Daddy was fading. He was talking randomly and drifting off.

"Letta, sometimes we do what we think is right and best at the time, and we do what we believe is best for those we love…" Carl said as he drifted out. Letta got a chill down her spine…she knew what her father was trying to say - about what they had done almost 30 years ago - the decisions they had made that changed the course of her life and Thomi's and potentially, William's. She KNEW what he was saying but in her heart, she never blamed HIM.

Letta stepped into the hall and asked the doctor to be honest with her about the prognosis. Dr. Wallace, one of the best cardiologists in the state, explained to Carletta that Carl had suffered two quick heart attacks, and that his heart was still "in shock" and not responding to medication. They decided not to do surgery because of his age. Had he considered preventative surgery a couple of years ago, maybe things would be different now. The doctor said it was basically a "wait and see" game at this point. If he doesn't respond soon, the family will need to make some decisions. Letta's heart shattered. She thanked him and went to the Chapel with Uncle B.

Letta kneeled down, and before she could start to pray, she started to cry. "God, Uncle B - I LOVE my Daddy so much, I can't make it without him. I know we live across the world from each other, but my Daddy has always been there - just a phone call away. Uncle B! I don't know if I…"

"Hush, baby, hush. You can do anything God leads you to do. God is a good father, too. He is everything you need and will give you the strength to handle whatever comes your way."

Letta couldn't help but feel that Uncle B was talking about something much deeper than he was actually saying. At that moment, the weight of everything was so heavy she couldn't carry the secret anymore.

"You know about Thomi - don't you? You and Aunt Carrie know?"

"Yes, we know, and have known since Day 1," Uncle B said. "We did what Naomi and Carl wanted. We loved you, and we all wanted what was best for you. Thomas had a good upbringing - Carl and Oni gave him only the best - you know that. But to tell you the truth, niece - I have been thinking about it for a while. It's like God has put it on my mind....and I truly believe the Lord has put it on Carl's - to speak it - while he still can."

11.

The Vanishing of Secrets

Almost everyone in the tri-parish area turned out to pay their respects to Carl Douglas of Douglas House. Naomi was her ever-classy, bou-gee self looking immaculate just as Carl would have wanted. Everyone said nice things about him and raved about his character, his spirit, and his amazing voice. Carl was a great man with a good heart. He would be missed.

Sisters from the Eastern Star Sisterhood were clearing everything from the kitchen as Letta came in. "Carletta, you look so good, girl! I love your hair. You know everybody used to say you looked just like Ms. Charlotte. Just beautiful with beautiful hair! We used to tease Naomi Faye about how she had given Ms. Charlotte a baby because you never looked like your mom...you look just like your Grandmother, chile! That's why your daddy was so crazy about you. I remember when you were born. He already had your name picked out. Naomi Faye wanted to name you Virginia, but Carl laid down the law! He insisted that you would be Carletta, and that was that! Yes, chile, he loved you most of all."

Naomi Faye - that was a name that Letta hadn't heard in a lifetime! Naomi would faint if she heard herself being referred to as "Naomi Faye." She was Naomi!

Letta made her way out to the veranda. Frei and Thomi were on the porch with their new baby girl. Emerald was so pretty and already had tiny earrings. Thomi loved his baby girl! She was beautiful and had Frei's eyes.

Letta hugged Thomi and asked if he was alright. "Yes, I'm good - how about you?" She wondered how her son was really doing. He had lost the only father he had ever known. Letta wondered if he deserved a chance to know the truth but couldn't bring herself to say the words. Instead she searched his face restlessly to see if she could discern how he was really doing.

"I'm hanging in there," she said, "Just worried about you and Oni. Does Mom look okay?"

"She is Naomi Boudreaux Douglas. Of course, she is alright. She knows how to act. Tonight may be a different story, though. Are y'all staying with her? Frei and I and Em are going over to Frei's parent's house. What about you and Trey? Where is he anyway?"

Letta hadn't noticed that she had not seen Trey in a while. She looked for him everywhere and finally found him in the backyard, almost down to the deck. Letta called for him. He waved her down, and she met him halfway. He took her hand - he had always been as sweet as his father - and as they walked, he said to her, "Ma, G-Pop loved you more than anything. He used to tell me that and he used to tell me to take care of you because life had not been kind to you but that you were a good woman - a strong woman - and he wanted to make sure I knew that. He told me, Mom - everything - about Grand Naomi and about Thomi's dad, Malcolm Thomas. I know everything, Mom, G-Pop told me last year during Easter. I promised I would not say anything until YOU were ready. I LOVE Uncle Thomi, and knowing he is my big brother just makes me so happy I feel like I might burst and I know he feels the same way!"

Letta was speechless. Trey hugged her and told her, "I love you, Mom, I know what happened, and I understand why. G-Pop made sure of it."

"Did you tell your Dad? Does Thomi know?" Letta was in shock. Who else knew? It was finally over! This wicked web of deceit that had been woven almost 35 years ago was "fully spun" and it was time to tear it down.

Letta made a conscious decision - she had to get it out - that's what her Daddy was trying to let her know - that it was okay and it was TIME. Before she left Ford County it would be all out. How ironic that in the place where "it" all started, it would end, and the wicked web that was spun would be over.

Later, after she had absorbed everything, Letta called Thomi at the Marshall's.

"Hey Sis, everything okay?"

"Thomas -"

"Uh oh, you said, 'Thomas.' This is serious," he joked.

"Yes, it is serious. I need to see you and Frei tonight at about 8:00. Everything is okay. I just want to share some things with you both that are long overdue."

— • ◆ • —

Letta had practiced this a million times - when it would finally come down to this minute, she knew what she needed and wanted to say. Frei and Thomi were prompt. Naomi was resting in bed. William and Trey were packing the Rover and getting everything ready to head home tomorrow morning. Letta asked everyone to come into the kitchen.

She was numb as she began the speech she had rehearsed in her head for ages. She began by saying how she never meant to hurt anyone and explaining that the disappointment and disgrace that she had caused was so overwhelming that she didn't know what to do - so she did nothing - and that's how the web of deceit got out of control. Her Daddy's dying wish was that she end it, and now she must. Naomi knew what was coming next.

Trey got up and stood by his Mom. "Mom, let me. I know I can explain it just like G-Pop explained to me." Both William's and Thomi's eyes were wide as saucers. What on earth was he talking about?

He looked at his father and uncle and said, "Dad, Uncle Thomas, a long time ago, things happened in Mom's life - the actions were her own - the consequences and actions afterwards were those of others and not her fault. Uncle Thomas, I have known for a long time now that you are my brother and my mom is your mom. I know about your real dad, Malcolm Thomas. I know about Aunt BethMae and how she helped mom have you in Cheneaux County. G-Pop told me everything last Easter. He knew he was sick, but Grand Naomi didn't. He

wanted me and Uncle Thomi to know the truth about what happened and why and I'm just excited to know I have a brother!"

William turned to Letta with tears in his eyes. "Letta, you could have told me. You had to know that I suspected it. I left the door open for you many times - were you just that scared, baby? Why? I love you, and I knew you came from a different world than mine. I knew there were certain things you had to do and certain ways you had to act - Carl told me that long ago, the first Christmas we spent with them. He assured me that in your OWN time, you would let me in." He hugged Letta - like no other hug she had ever received, and Letta broke down and sobbed in his arms. She was finally free!

Naomi stared silently into space. "Mother, I had to get it out. I had to," said Letta. Oni just hugged Letta with all her strength and asked her to please forgive her because, at the time, she really DID believe it was the right thing to do - for everyone.

Thomas was sitting there - looking at Trey with tears in his eyes. All he could do was grab Trey and hug him as tight as he could without taking his breath away. He had found his brother - the part of him that was missing, and he was never letting him go!

It was alright, everything WAS alright, just as Aunt BethMae had told Letta over 30 years ago. Everything always really WOULD be alright!

12.

God's Will Be Done

Letta and William were preparing for Trey's graduation from Howard University. Letta was excited that she would finally have her baby boy back at home. It had been almost 8 years, and she missed Trey terribly while he was away at college. William was in the process of hiring two new attorneys at the firm. His father had completely retired, and William was heading the law firm - the first Black law firm in the city, which his Dad had established almost 35 years ago. Trey would come on as an intern to learn the ropes, and eventually, he would work side by side with his Dad, just as William had done with his Dad. All was well with the Langston family and with everything that Letta had been through in her lifetime, she had learned that God was still good and ever-present. She vowed to herself to never let secrets separate her from those she loved ever again and not to lose any more precious time with her mother, her sons, and her grandsons.

Well, that was a good thing because things were about to get a little complicated and that wicked web that was woven way back in the day was about to rear its ugly head.

Frei and Thomi were flying in for Trey's graduation. Emerald could not ride in a car for more than two hours before getting car sick, so they decided flying was the best thing to do. Naomi was NOT a fan of flying, but Emerald convinced her "Grand Naomi" that flying was the best thing so they could have more time to spend with Letta, William, and Trey.

The graduation was extraordinary. Seeing Trey get "hooded" was the most wonderful experience and fulfilled every dream Letta had anticipated for her baby boy for a long time. Having a law degree would take Trey far, and Letta knew he would be successful, especially with his Dad to guide and mentor him. "Ooooo, baby, you look so handsome in your Master's Hood! I am so proud of you!"

Letta was beaming, and so was William. In fact, William was a little "teary-eyed." He was just so proud of his son! As they were walking to the car, Trey let his parents know that he had "someone" he wanted them to meet. Letta had a semi-frown on her brow because she just knew it was a girl, and she WAS not ready for that! Trey stated that he and his friend would be flying back to Boston in a few days so that they could get things tied up and get their luggage shipped home. He told everyone to go on ahead to the reception, and he would find his friend and meet them there.

As they were walking to Bethune Hall for the reception, Naomi - walking between Frei and Letta, arm in arm - stated that she was so blessed and so happy to see her family grow and become so successful - she wished Carl was here to see this time. It had been almost ten years since Carl's passing but, Naomi confessed, to her it was like yesterday. She still missed him so terribly much.

Thomi and William had gotten very close over the years. They often talked over the phone about family and work. Thomi looked up to William and respected him. He called him "Dad," and that made William very proud. Thomi was one of the top headhunters in Atlanta and Frei was very happy working with special needs children. With Emerald being a teenager, this work gave Frei purpose and fulfilled her life immensely. Emerald was learning to drive - that was her Dad's bright idea - but it was practical since he traveled so much, and Frei did not have the nerves to teach Emmy how to drive. Emmy was definitely the "apple" of her Dad's eye, and she could get anything from her "Big Daddy" William. Letta could see so much of herself in Emmy - her only grandchild - she could hardly believe it!

William and Thomi were chatting over by the stage when Thomi noticed Trey come into the reception hall. Thomi nudged William, "There's Trey and his friend. At least it's a boy, so Mom (Naomi was still "Momma," but Letta was MOM) won't have a fit." They laughed and anticipated the news that Trey had to tell them.

Trey introduced his friend as "Mal." He was from Birmingham, but he came to Howard to be close to his father, who was an activist and professor at Howard. Everyone was glad to meet "Mal," and Naomi quickly asked about his family back in Birmingham. She was very curious about "Mal" and his family, and so was Letta.

"Well, ma'am, I grew up in Birmingham with my mother and my grandparents. My grandfather was the president of Morgan Bank & Trust, but he died four years ago. My grandmother was a teacher at Alabama State for a very long time, but when she retired, she moved back to Ford County to be near my mother. Trey told me you guys were from Ford County, too. Wow, what a small world, huh?"

When Naomi heard Morgan Bank & Trust, her eyebrow heightened, and Letta almost turned white. Neither said a word! The look on their faces verified what they both were thinking. Oh Lord, is this Thomi's brother..is this Malcolm's son? Did Trey and Mal already figure that out and that's why Trey wanted Mal to come and meet his family?

On the way to the airport, William and Thomi were discussing what they were going to do when they got back to Boston. William had a couple business partners he wanted Thomi to meet, and Thomi was excited about the possibility of forming a business relationship with them. Neither William nor Thomi had a clue what had just taken place at Bethune Hall - but Naomi and Letta knew, and both of them KNEW they had to get to the bottom of Trey's new friend.

"What time does our flight get back, William," Letta asked, "I thought we'd just go out to eat since everyone will be tired, and I know I will NOT be doing any cooking! I'll call and make reservations when we land."

"Sure, Babe, that's fine," William said, "I could go for some Italian. Call Giovanni's. We can go there. I know Naomi will like that."

Naomi was somewhere - way back in time - thinking about what happened in 1961. Was that wicked web back? She didn't respond to William's comment which let Letta KNOW where she was and what she was thinking about. What had Trey and his friend talked about and for how long?

When Trey saw Thomi coming through the terminal, he was excited. "Hey man, I didn't know you guys were staying after graduation. I figured Grand Naomi wanted to get back to Douglas House - I know she hates being away from home. Where's Dad? Didn't he come with you?"

"Yeah," said Thomi, "he's waiting outside. You know he did not want to park, so he's waiting just outside the terminal." When they got outside the airport Trey was admiring a slick little BMW convertible that was parked outside - it was HOT! The thing that caught Trey's eye was that his DAD was behind the wheel.

Trey called to let his father know he would be flying in tomorrow and wanted him to have a rental car waiting for him. William told him that he and Thomi would pick him up from the airport, and he did not need a rental. Trey was okay with that.

"Hey, Dad! So you decided to give up the Rover and go "fly" like the young cats, huh?"

William laughed and said, "No, my boy, I will always be a "Rover" man, but like you said, the young cats are driving Beamers and since you are a young cat, I guess this is for you."

"GET outta HERE!!!! Dad, are you serious? Thom, don't y'all be playing with me! Dad! For real?!??"

"Yes, Trey. For real, your Mom picked it out." Trey jumped into his Beamer and just screamed. William and Thomi were laughing and just enjoying Trey's reaction.

Meanwhile, Frei and Emerald were about to go shopping. Emerald asked her grandmomma Letta if she wanted to join them. "Mom promised me that we could go shopping," said Emmy, "so we have to leave before Dad and Big Daddy get back. Y'all coming?"

"No Emmy, baby. Y'all go ahead. Me and your GG Naomi are gonna rest and get ready for dinner."

Frei and Emerald left with Emmy begging to drive, and Frei adamantly saying "NO!"

Naomi watched them from the large kitchen bay window as Letta was getting them a cold drink. Without looking at Letta, Naomi asked, "How in the world did that happen? After all these years, why would God let this happen? Do you think they talked about anything else, Carletta, Lord have mercy!"

Letta was nervous and had to take a shot of cognac to ease her nerves. "Okay, Mother, calm down. Let's think. Do you really think that's Malcolm Thomas' son?"

"Hell YES," commanded Naomi, "I know it is, and so do you, Letta! I remember when Britton Thomas got that position at Morgan Bank & Trust - it was all over the news. During that time, that was a BIG deal for a Black man to have such a prestigious position. We BOTH know that "Mal" is Malcolm's son and Thomi's BROTHER!"

"What should we do Letta? I am so tired. I never thought we would have to deal with this again. But as my dear sister, BethMae would say, what's done in the dark …"

"OK, MOTHER, we must deal with this, but how? I need to talk to William first - I need to tell him our suspicions - he will know how to handle it."

Thomi had packed the Rover, and they were ready to head to the airport and back to Ford County when Trey came out to the car. "Well, big brother, I guess I will see you guys for Christmas. I am so glad that y'all were here for my graduation. My niece Emerald is so beautiful - you and Frei have your hands full - but she's a good kid - she looks like Mom a lot." Thomi hugged Trey and told him he loved him very much and that he was proud of him.

"Okay, guys, the plane is not going to wait for y'all, so we need to get to the airport," said Letta.

"I'll call you, Mother, tonight. We can talk then. Tell Victoria I said hello." Victoria was the young lady that stayed with Naomi. Since Carl's passing, Naomi had taken in a roommate. Douglas House was so big, and Naomi was lonesome there alone. Frei interviewed Victoria and about a hundred others, but she decided that Victoria and Naomi were a perfect match, and she was right. With Victoria there, she and Thomi did not worry about Naomi being by herself. Although they were just four hours away, they still did not want Naomi to be alone at Douglas House, and Victoria was her perfect companion. She was studying nursing at the local college, and she was very attentive to Naomi.

Naomi heard the phone and knew it was Carletta. Victoria answered and quickly called her to the phone, "Miss Naomi, it's Miss Letta. I'll bring you the phone." Naomi was lying on her chaise in the study anticipating Letta's call and thinking about what she would say. "Yes, Mother, you are right. I know," confirmed Letta, "Yes, we should tell everyone - the sooner, the better. One good thing is that Trey and Thomi already knew the story of Malcolm Thomas - which would lessen the blow - hopefully. Lord have mercy!"

Almost a month had passed, and Letta had not said anything to William or Trey about "Mal." That night, Trey came up to his parent's bedroom and informed them that "Mal" had a job interview near Boston and was flying up on Friday. He asked if maybe "Mal" could stay with them for the weekend because he and Trey had a lot of catching up to do.

Letta said, "Let me and your Dad talk about it, and we'll let you know."

"Mom, it's not like we don't have the room. What's up?"

"William…," when he was "William" and not "Trey" that usually meant there was some sort of problem. "Your Father and I will let you know, okay?"

"Okay, sure, Mother, that's fine. Let me know so I can tell "Mal."

William looked at Carletta, "Is there something we need to talk about, Baby? "Mal" seems like a nice young man, and he and Trey are close. It's okay with me if he wants to spend the weekend - we have six bedrooms - so we DO have room. Letta pulled her beautiful natural locks back into a ponytail.

"Yes, I know that, William, but what you don't know is…" Letta was interrupted by the phone.

Trey had gotten it downstairs and was yelling up, "Mom, it's Victoria! Get the phone. I'll be back in a minute."

13.

By God's Grace

***

"Hello Mother, is everything okay?"

Naomi sounded good and strong, "Yes, Daughter, all is well. The funny thing is, I saw Madelyn B at Lilly Rubin's the other day - you know everyone down here is getting ready for the Cotillion (don't you miss that Honey)?"

"Are you serious? Of course not!" Letta thought.

"Madelyn looks great," Naomi continued, "Well, you know we were talking about our kids and grandkids and stuff, and she mentioned that Malcolm and his wife had moved back to Atlanta and that their son, Mal, was coming back there to work because he got a teaching job at Clark. Isn't that great?"

Letta was beside herself. "So Mother, are you confirming that Mal is Malcolm Thomas' son? Is that what you are trying to tell me?"

Oni, sighed and said, "Chile, that's what I'm saying, but I am also saying that he is not his "natural" Father. I got the scoop from Victoria. You know she knows everything that goes on here!"

Letta released some tension and asked, "Well, Mother, what EXACTLY did Victoria say?"

Naomi was about 87 years old now, and her memory was very sporadic. Her chain of thought was horrible, and it was definitely testing Carletta's patience.

"Did you see Emerald's shots in Essence? We are so proud of her, and you know my Great-Grand baby is the talk of the South! Everyone knows she is a "Douglas," an offspring of The Douglases of Ford County, chile!"

"MOTHER!" Letta almost screamed, "What were you saying about Malcolm and his son?"

"Well, chile, Victoria said that Malcolm is a Thomas, but he is NOT Malcolm's son. He is actually Nathaniel's son, Malcolm's oldest brother. The sad thing you know is that Nate was killed about 12 maybe 15 years ago, and later on, Malcolm married the girl, so actually, Mal is Thomi's cousin, NOT his brother. What a blessing! Yes, I told Madelyn by the Grace of God, it seems that everything does work out for the good of all. Just like my wise sister BethMae would say, everything WILL be alright."

After that exhausting conversation with her mother, Letta hung up the phone and just got on her knees and prayed for all the things that God had done and how he had protected her again and again. She was so relieved and so grateful that the web REALLY was over and she could be at peace with her life.

Letta called Trey and asked him why he did not tell her about Mal, who he really was and without hesitation, Trey said he and Mal had talked about the past and after that, he just remembered what his G-Pop said before he passed away, that everything happens for a reason and that no matter what the situation, God would make it alright and he was right ...everything was all right ...

Carletta hung up the phone with a peaceful smile on her face. Yes, indeed, what a wicked web we weave, when we practice to deceive...but faith and grace DOES make everything all right!

The End